Samuel French Acting Edition

I0591860

Kill Local

by Mat Smart

SAMUELFRENCH.COM   SAMUELFRENCH.CO.UK

FOR PRODUCTION ENQUIRIES

UNITED STATES AND CANADA
Info@SamuelFrench.com
1-866-598-8449

UNITED KINGDOM AND EUROPE
Plays@SamuelFrench.co.uk
020-7255-4302

Each title is subject to availability from Samuel French, depending
upon country of performance. Please be aware that *KILL LOCAL* may
not be licensed by Samuel French in your territory. Professional and
amateur producers should contact the nearest Samuel French office or
licensing partner to verify availability.

MUSIC USE NOTE

Licensees are solely responsible for obtaining formal written permission from copyright owners to use copyrighted music in the performance of this play and are strongly cautioned to do so. If no such permission is obtained by the licensee, then the licensee must use only original music that the licensee owns and controls. Licensees are solely responsible and liable for all music clearances and shall indemnify the copyright owners of the play(s) and their licensing agent, Samuel French, against any costs, expenses, losses and liabilities arising from the use of music by licensees. Please contact the appropriate music licensing authority in your territory for the rights to any incidental music.

IMPORTANT BILLING AND CREDIT REQUIREMENTS

If you have obtained performance rights to this title, please refer to your licensing agreement for important billing and credit requirements.

KILL LOCAL premiered at La Jolla Playhouse (Artistic Director, Christopher Ashley; Managing Director, Michael S. Rosenberg) in La Jolla, California on August 6, 2017. The performance was directed by Jackson Gay, with scenic design by Wilson Chin, costume design by Jessica Ford, lighting design by Paul Whitaker, sound design by Broken Chord, fight direction by Steve Rankin, and casting by Telsey + Company; Karyn Casl, C.S.A. The dramaturg was Shirley Fishman, and the stage manager was Rob Chikar. The cast was as follows:

TODD . . . . Matthew Amendt

SHEILA . . . . Amanda Quaid

ABI . . . . Xochitl Romero

GLORIA . . . . Candy Buckley

AMI . . . . Carolyn Braver

KILL LOCAL was developed in La Jolla Playhouse's DNA New Works Series.

It was originally written and developed in the Dorothy Strelsin New American Writers Group at Primary Stages.

It also received a developmental reading at SPACE on Ryder Farm and a workshop at the University of Evansville.

CHARACTERS

TODD – early thirties
SHEILA – early thirties
ABI – late twenties, Sheila's sister
GLORIA – fifties or older, Sheila and Abi's mother
AMI – seventeen years old

AUTHOR'S NOTE

There is an intermission between Act One and Act Two.

SPECIAL THANKS

Michelle Bossy, for her leadership, insights, and belief in this play.

Jaime Castañeda, Gabriel Greene, and Teresa Sapien, for their advocacy and friendship over the years.

For my sisters, Tifanie and Karen

ACT ONE

(An unfinished floor in an unfinished high-rise building. The construction site has been abandoned.)

(Some of the windows are windows, some are covered in sheets of plastic that breathe in and out with the wind. Sunlight pours in from outside. It is noon.)

(There are dozens of bags of fast-setting concrete mix, a few tarps, a wheelbarrow, a water hose, and other random construction materials. The insulation and wires of the walls are exposed. Work lights hang from the ceiling. There are a couple of folding chairs strewn about.)

(One section of the floor does not have the concrete poured yet. A few steel reinforcement bars and plumbing pipes run through it.)

*(***TODD***'s hands are tied together and his arms are pulled above him with a rope that hangs from a metal beam. He is hoisted above the section of floor without concrete. His feet barely touch the exposed bars and pipes. His knees and ankles are zip-tied. His phone, keys, wallet, and fountain pen are thrown to the side.)*

*(Nearby, ***SHEILA*** sits on a folding chair on the finished section of the floor. She has a 9mm Beretta holstered to her hip. She wears gloves.*

*She plays Bejeweled on her phone with the
sound on.* This goes on for a while.)*

TODD. I knew you didn't seem like an investor. I knew I
   shouldn't have done a tour of the building myself, but
   you insisted and your financials looked great and you
   look great – so I said, "Sure. Sure, Meredith, come on
   over – I'll show you myself."
   Idiot!
   Is Meredith even your real name?
   Probably not. Your name is probably something like...
   Sloan. Or Braxtyn. With a t y n at the end. Are you a
   fucking Braxtyn?

   *(**SHEILA** continues to play Bejeweled.)*

   Who are you?

   (Beat.)

   What are you waiting for, hm?

   (Beat.)

   Who hired you?

   (Beat.)

   I demand answers!

   (Beat.)

   You can't just leave me hanging here.

   (He laughs. **SHEILA** *doesn't. She continues to
   play Bejeweled.)*

   ...Not quite cold enough for gloves yet, is it?

   (Beat.)

   Are those the gloves with those special fingertips that
   work on screens?
   I tried a pair once and they didn't work. But those look
   like they're working pretty well for you.

---

*A license to produce *Kill Local* does not include a performance license
for any third-party or copyrighted recordings. Licensees should create
their own original video game soundscape for use in their productions.

What brand are they?

Maybe you could just hold them up? – so I can see the brand?

I want to put them on my Christmas list. You can never start too early.

> *(Without looking at him,* **SHEILA** *makes a face that says, "I think you can start too early sometimes." She continues to play.)*

It's not cold enough for gloves yet.

> *(He starts to hyperventilate. He tries to calm himself down by speaking.)*

Do you say fall or autumn?

My mother said autumn. She made it sound so regal.

"Autumn is my favorite time of the year," she'd say.

"Oh, I just love autumn, Toddley."

My full name is Todd – I mean, Todd's not short for anything – Todd's just Todd – but she'd sometimes call me Toddley – just for kicks. God, I miss her.

My parents died last year. The terrible pileup on 495. Twelve people died. It was just terrible. Everything changed that day and I –

> *(His hyperventilating gets worse. He holds his breath and tries to get himself back under control.)*

Are you playing Bejeweled?

> *(***SHEILA*** *continues to play Bejeweled.)*

Are you playing Bejeweled?

> *(***SHEILA*** *continues to play Bejeweled.)*

Are you playing fucking Bejeweled before you kill me? Before you kill me in my own building? – is that what this is?

> *(***SHEILA*** *continues to play Bejeweled.)*

How can you just – what kind of person could – are you really playing Bejeweled right now?

SHEILA. Yes.

TODD. I'm more of a Tetris guy.

> (**SHEILA** *looks at him for the first time. A judgment.*)

God, my head is – how did you –

Was that chloroform?

SHEILA. Chloroform takes five minutes to knock someone out.

TODD. So what was that?

SHEILA. Something quicker.

> (*She pauses her game and makes a call. She puts in a Bluetooth earpiece. She waits.*)

TODD. Who are you calling now?

> (*The person on the other end of the call answers.* **SHEILA** *only speaks into the phone through her Bluetooth, not to* **TODD**.)

SHEILA. Do I have the G. O. yet? Mom's been ignoring my calls.

TODD. You've been calling your mother?

SHEILA. Did we get the final wire yet?

TODD. What is this? – a *family* business?

SHEILA. What is taking so long?

(Turning away, quietly.) He's already awake.

Yeah, I didn't think it'd take this long, so I didn't even bring any duct tape and now he's just –

> (*She speaks in a funny voice, not unlike the adults in* Peanuts, *to mock Todd. Her words are indecipherable.*)

I don't know, there's probably something I could stuff in there.

> *(Beat.)*

Um… I'll have a burrito bowl.

What's that meat called?

No, not steak.

Yeah, carnitas.

TODD. You're ordering lunch?

SHEILA. With the corn salsa. Extra guac.

Okay, fine – regular guac.

TODD. You're ordering lunch!

SHEILA. You made sure the water is on here, right?

TODD. What do you need water for?

Are you going to waterboard me?

> *(He starts looking around.)*

SHEILA. Just have Mom call me when it's a G. O.

TODD. Oh, God – you need it to mix the concrete – oh, God! – are you going to bury me in the floor of my own building?

SHEILA. *(To* **TODD.***)* Zip it.

(On phone.) No – nothing happened. I just – on the way here I saw Tara Hutchinson at the gas station – with her two little girls and I –

I can't talk about it now.

> *(She goes to a corner and turns away from* **TODD.***)*

I don't know – later. Sometime when Mom's not around. Mom's not always around.

(Lowering her voice.) I just don't know how much…joy I get from this anymore.

But I don't know what else I'd do – what would I do?

And I don't even know if I could turn this off.

If there was a pill I could take to make myself stop, I would take it.

I mean – if some random guy is rude to the cashier at the CVS, I follow him and think of a thousand different ways I could kill him without anyone ever finding out.

This is what I was born to do.

It's what Mom was born to do.

Abi, please don't make this about you. You're good at what you do.

You're great, okay? You're amazing. But you're in the office. You're not out here pulling the trigger.

TODD. Excuse me, I –

SHEILA. I just thought there would come a time when we could *enjoy* this. But no, we constantly have to scrape and claw for the few jobs that are out there. And no matter how good we are, we practically lose everything to Greystone or China or the CIA. It is such a grind – all the time – and the constant training –

TODD. I really need to use the bathroom.

SHEILA. And it used to all be worth it: to get paid to put a bullet into the head of some scumbag. Not knowing if it'd be a clean entry/exit through the skull, no mess – or if it'd be like an exploding watermelon. But now I just hope for a sniper shot or a poisoning – something where I don't have to worry about cleaning up the splatter.

TODD. *(To himself.)* I'm gonna piss my pants.

SHEILA. I used to love the splatter.

TODD. Oh, God.

SHEILA. And listening to a human being's last breaths?

But you do it enough times and you get used to it.

But great work – the great work – shouldn't it always feel new and dangerous?

Or have *I* lost what made it great?

> *(**TODD** wets himself. **SHEILA** turns back to him and watches.)*

...I should go.

Yeah.

Yeah.

Yeah.

Bye.

(She hangs up.)

(To **TODD**.*)* Really?

TODD. Sorry, I –

I, um, coincidentally – I ate an early lunch at Chipotle today – and I had like three refills of Diet Coke. When there's free refills, I drink it like it's water. It's a problem.

> (**TODD** *and* **SHEILA** *watch the urine soak through his pants.)*

I'm never having Diet Coke again. It goes right through me.

(A realization.) I am never having Diet Coke again.

> *(He starts to cry.)*

So this is how it ends. Much like it began. I was a bedwetter – up until my freshman year of high school.

I guess everything comes full circle.

> *(Beat.)*

But you know what? I have never broken the law. What I did wasn't popular, but it was one hundred percent legal. If anyone has a problem with the way I have conducted business here, they need to take it up with Congress. Not hire a goddamned hitman.

SHEILA. I'm not a man.

TODD. Who hired you? Was it Vincent?

Was it the Serbs? Or Representative Binkley?

I mean, to shoot me and bury me in the concrete of my own building? – that's some Old Testament shit.

...The Teachers' Union! Those retirement fund reps for the Teachers' Union are fucking cutthroat – did they hire you?

SHEILA. "In capitalism, the question of morality is answered by asking only one thing:

Will someone pay for it?"

Do you remember saying that?

TODD. I don't remember a day, in recent memory, that I didn't say it.

SHEILA. So. Full circle.

TODD. Whatever whoever is paying you, I will double it. I'll triple it.

SHEILA. The only way we're still in business is that we have integrity.

TODD. You are not qualified to talk about integrity, murderer.

(Beat.)

I can still get this building finished. I can get everyone's investments back. If this is only about money, I –

SHEILA. This is about right and wrong.

(Beat.)

And money.

You wanted this building to fail.

You wanted to wreck people's lives to make your own life better.

TODD. Yeah, but at least I don't kill people.

You people and your guns are wrecking our country.

"Get all the guns! Get all the guns and Melt Them Down. I don't give a shit about the Second Amendment."

*(**SHEILA** laughs.)*

I have over a thousand dollars in my wallet. I'll pay you that to run your hands through my hair. What do you say?

Who are we to judge if it's right or wrong? As long as someone will pay for it.

*(**SHEILA**'s phone rings. The sound makes **TODD** jump. After a couple of rings, **SHEILA** answers it.)*

SHEILA. Yeah.

Yeah.

Yeah.

Yeah, no – no lettuce.

TODD. *(To himself.)* Oh –

SHEILA. Just the corn salsa stuff and guac on the side.
Did I say cheese?

(To **TODD**.*)* Did I ever say cheese? Did I?

TODD. No.

SHEILA. *(Into the Bluetooth.)* I never said cheese.

> *(She takes out her gun and puts a silencer on it.)*

No, I am not lactose intolerant, I'm just trying not to pump my system with saturated fat like you do.
No, Mom hasn't called me yet, okay? You do your job, I'll do mine.

> *(She hangs up.)*

TODD. You should try a burrito quesadilla. It's what I had. It's a burrito, but instead of using just a flour tortilla to wrap it in, they wrap it in a quesadilla.

SHEILA. *(Snapping.)* I'm watching my carbs.

TODD. Oh, you are – are you? I fucking hate people who watch their carbs.
My sister is doing the gluten-free thing now and it makes eating with her a total pain in the ass.

SHEILA. You don't have a sister.

TODD. I have a half-sister.

SHEILA. You don't have any brothers or sisters. Neither did your parents. All four of your grandparents are dead. You are –

TODD. All alone? I thought I was.
But at my father's funeral – boom – there she is: "I'm your sister."

SHEILA. Bullshit.

TODD. Turns out a long time ago my dad had an affair – got this woman pregnant – and my mom forbade him from having anything to do with this bastard daughter. He never even met her – but he gave her half the company. He gave this unknown half-sister half the company.

The company I have put my whole life into.

A final "fuck you" from the grave – Love, Dad.

If you think I'm a snake, you should've met my father. He had venom running through his veins.

(To the heavens.) You happy, Dad? You happy you were right about me? That I'm a wussy? That I'm a bedwetter?

Fuck you, Dad! – fuck you!

Thank you!

Fuck you!

(To **SHEILA**.*)* Can I call my sister?

Please let me call my sister.

SHEILA. You heard me talking to my sister and so you invented a sister.

TODD. I swear to God it's the truth. Please let me call her.

SHEILA. Not gonna happen.

TODD. We had a big fight the last time we saw each other. I need to set things straight with her. Please let me call her. Wouldn't you want that chance? – to set things straight with your sister before you die. Please.

> *(Beat.)*

What's your real name?

You're going to kill me, right? Will you at least tell me your real name?

> *(Beat.)*

My sister and I have only known each other for a year – and I hated her at first, but then something funny happened:

I started to not mind having her around. Half-Full.

We, uh – we like to play games with each other like we're kids. To make up for lost time.

We like to play Pillow Fart.

We like to play Embrace the Suck. Have you ever played? It's when – when things suck – you embrace it.

You wanna play? I'll go first.

(He takes a deep breath in – and then out.)

It sucks that you're gonna kill me.

It sucks that I prolly deserve it.

It sucks that you're hot and we're meeting under these circumstances. Your turn.

(Beat.)

You pass? Okay, I'll go again.

I did want this building to fail.

I have done this over and over. In twelve different states. In five different countries.

I have robbed hundreds of people of their life's savings.

And I have enjoyed doing it. And that sucks.

That's the part of me I got from my dad.

But you know what? I've also got a lot of my mom in me, too.

And after she died, I couldn't look myself in the mirror anymore. I was ashamed. I wasn't the man my mother wanted me to be.

And I thought it was too late for me to change, but my sister...she convinced me to start showing this property to investors again. No more non-recourse loans. That's why I showed it to you.

I am trying to fix this. I am.

If you want to stop doing this, you can.

And I understand that I have to pay for what I did – but also, whoever hired you wants the old Todd dead. But he's already gone.

I no longer sit down and think: How can I take everything this person owns?

I think: How can we make a deal where we both win?

How can we do that?

How can I help you turn this off?

(Beat.)

SHEILA. You are who you are, Todd McIntyre.

I am who I am.

TODD. What is your name?

SHEILA. I am going to kill you.

TODD. I know.

SHEILA. ...Sheila.

TODD. ...Sheila.

      (*Beat.* **SHEILA** *runs her hands through his hair.*)

...If there is a God, please let me stop being Todd McIntyre.

And please, God, let you not be Sheila.

Let you be Meredith again. Be an investor who can help me right this wrong.

You are not stuck.

No matter what you think, we are never stuck.

Please let me call my sister.

SHEILA. ...No.

TODD. Then please, at least, write down her number. And one day, if you have any shred of decency left in your cold, murderous heart – please tell her that I said:

I'm sorry.

That I love her.

That she is not alone because she is brave. And resourceful. And twice as smart as me.

And ask her:

What do you get when you take a glass half-empty and add it to a glass half-full?

      (*Beat.*)

She'll know what it means.

There's some paper right there. My pen is on the floor. Please just write down her number.

      (**SHEILA** *picks up the piece of paper. She picks up Todd's fountain pen.*)

SHEILA. Nice pen.

TODD. It's a seven-hundred-dollar pen.

SHEILA. What is it?

TODD. It's a Montblanc.

SHEILA. No – what's her number?

TODD. It's – shit. It's in my phone. You can look it up on my phone.

SHEILA. I'm not turning on your phone.

TODD. It's 7-2-6. Then it's – it's – dammit. Please just let me look it up on my phone.

SHEILA. Either you're going to remember it or –

> *(Her phone rings. It's loud, startling – a different ring than before.* **TODD** *jumps. He inadvertently lets out a small, scared yelp.)*
>
> *(The phone rings again.)*
>
> (**SHEILA** *and* **TODD** *stare at each other.)*
>
> *(The phone rings a third time.)*

TODD. 726-324-6644.

> (**SHEILA** *writes down the number on the paper.)*
>
> *(Her phone rings a fourth time. She answers it.)*

SHEILA. Yeah.
  Yeah.
  Yeah, Mom. Got it.

> *(She hangs up. She picks up her gun.)*

TODD. Name your price. Anything.

> (**SHEILA** *takes off the safety.)*

SHEILA. Three.

TODD. Three what? Three million?

SHEILA. Two.

TODD. Please let me be / the last person you kill.

SHEILA. / One.

> (**SHEILA** *shoots* **TODD** *in the head.)*
>
> *(His brain and skull splatter every which way. It's a mess.)*

(He slumps over, still hanging from the ropes.)

*(****SHEILA**** moves close and listens to the life leave him.)*

(She waits for his breath to stop.)

SHEILA. Oh, Toddley. I hope you are the last person I kill.

(She runs her hands through his bloody hair. A piece of his scalp sticks to her glove. She tries to shake it off. It sticks.)

Dammit.

(She shakes her hand until it comes off.)

*(She cuts the rope. ****TODD****'s body falls onto the unfinished floor.)*

(His arms are still above his head – in the same position he was in while hanging. It makes it so he won't fit into the floor.)

(She pushes his arms down to his sides.)

(She dials a number as she pushes him between the steel reinforcement bars and plumbing pipes.)

(Into the Bluetooth.) Hi. I'd like to make a change to an existing takeout order. It's under my sister's name, Abi. Yep, that's it. But instead of the carnitas burrito bowl, could you make it a carnitas burrito quesadilla? Yes, a quesarito. Yes, that's it. Thank you.

(She hangs up.)

*(She takes a photo of ****TODD****.)*

(She sends it.)

(Singing, quietly.)

She'll be comin' round the mountain when she comes
She'll be comin' round the mountain when she comes –

(She quietly continues humming the song, but not singing it.)

(She picks up a bag of fast-setting concrete mix and puts it down next to the wheelbarrow.)

*(**TODD***'s arms move back up above his head.)*

*(**SHEILA** stops humming. She stares at **TODD**.)*

(She pushes his arms back down. When she's convinced they'll stay down, she gets the water hose. She's about to rip open the concrete mix, but stops.)

(She picks of the piece of paper with the phone number on it.)

(She dials the number. She waits.)

(She waits.)

(She waits.)

(The voicemail picks up. She abruptly hangs up the phone.)

(Blackout.)

(An hour later.)

*(**SHEILA** has just finished pouring the wet concrete over Todd's body and smoothing out the surface of it with a two-by-four.)*

(She surveys her work.)

(Slowly, Todd's hands rise through the wet concrete.)

SHEILA. For God's sake.

(She tries to push Todd's hands back under the wet concrete. They slowly keep popping back up.)

(She hears a noise.)

(She somersaults behind a pile of construction materials.)

(She draws her gun and waits.)

(The stairway door opens.)

*(It is **ABI**. She carries a bag of Chipotle and various other gear.)*

ABI. Sheila?

(Beat.)

SHEILA. What – in the hell – are you doing here, Abi?

ABI. Chipotle delivery!

SHEILA. I almost blew your head off.

I heard someone on the stairs and thought – "I'm gonna kill Abi for not warning me."

ABI. Don't worry – the sensors are working. I just wanted to surprise you.

SHEILA. No. Bad idea – terrible idea.

What are you doing here? Get back to the office.

ABI. Wait, what is that?

SHEILA. Todd's hands. I hoisted his arms up while I was waiting for the G. O. and now I can't get them to stay down.

ABI. You better fix that.

SHEILA. I've been trying to!

ABI. That's like some Han Solo shit.

Mom's gonna freak out when she gets here if his hands are like that.

SHEILA. Why is Mom coming here?

ABI. She said she was coming here – and that I should too.

SHEILA. Why?

ABI. She told me to bring the intel equipment, pick up lunch, and that we'd rendezvous here – then we're going on a field trip.

SHEILA. The three of us? You never come out to the field.

ABI. I know, but I just said okay because she sounded so pissed.

SHEILA. I'm calling her.

ABI. She told me to tell you not to call her.

SHEILA. What is going on?

ABI. I don't know.

SHEILA. Don't touch anything, okay?

Okay?

ABI. Okay.

(**SHEILA** *goes to her tool bag.*)

I think they screwed up our order because this bag weighs like ten pounds.

SHEILA. I changed my order to a quesarito.

ABI. Wait, what? Is that the thing where they wrap your burrito in a quesadilla?

SHEILA. Yep.

(**ABI** *gasps.*)

ABI. That's like enough carbs for a week.

SHEILA. I know.

ABI. And all that cheese? You'll be so bloated.

What is going on with you? What happened with Tara Hutchinson this morning?

(**SHEILA** *takes out a hacksaw.*)

ABI. What are you doing?

SHEILA. What do you think?

ABI. *(Grossed out.)* Oh, really?

SHEILA. You got any other ideas? I've got to get this fixed before Mom gets here.

ABI. Couldn't you have tied his arms down to his body?

SHEILA. ...Yes. And I should have. But I didn't think of it. You want to help me pull him out, tie down his arms, and then re-do the concrete?

ABI. I have an MBA from Wharton. I don't do concrete. Just hack 'em off. I'll look this way.

> (*She turns the other direction.*)
>
> (**SHEILA** *leans over the wet concrete, trying not to step on it. She starts cutting off one of Todd's hands with the hacksaw.*)

(*More to herself than to* **SHEILA.**) I didn't think today could get any crappier

but now I gotta listen to you saw through a guy's arms.

SHEILA. Why's your day been crappy?

ABI. It was just this terrible thing with Best Buy. I don't want to talk about it.

SHEILA. What happened?

ABI. Just this epic screw-up with the three new computers. We were supposed to get all the spyware for free, but somehow it got messed up, so I spent *two-and-a-half hours* on the phone this morning with Best Buy customer service trying to get it straightened out. It was a nightmare.

SHEILA. How much is each subscription?

ABI. Like sixty bucks.

SHEILA. So why don't we just pay it?

ABI. It's the principle, La-La! They need to honor their –

SHEILA. How much did today's project pay?

ABI. A lot.

SHEILA. So don't sweat it.

ABI. But our overhead is through the roof. We're still in the red on the year –

> (**SHEILA** *gets one of Todd's hands off.*)

SHEILA. Got it!

> (**ABI** *looks.*)

ABI. Oh, gross –

> (**SHEILA** *pushes the hand down into the wet concrete.*)
>
> (*She starts sawing off Todd's other hand.* **ABI** *looks away again.*)

SHEILA. All I'm saying is:

Is it worth getting totally stressed out to save two hundred bucks?

ABI. They promised the spyware to us. You can't just let people go back on their promises.

SHEILA. You should let it go.

ABI. Letting it go would mean that they win. That big business wins again.

SHEILA. I think that's blowing it out of –

ABI. We are a small, family-owned and -operated business. We're the little engine that could.

And even with our track record, we *still* get paid seventy-five cents on the dollar compared to what hit*men* get paid.

SHEILA. It's getting better.

> (*She gets Todd's other hand off. She pushes it into the wet concrete. She takes a two-by-four and smooths out the surface.*)

ABI. We deserve equal pay for equal work.

We've never exposed a client. We guarantee each and every job.

If we promise we're gonna take out Todd McIntyre, then we take out Todd McIntyre.

Unlike *Best Buy*, we do the job we promise to do – always.

SHEILA. I think comparing us to Best Buy is apples and oranges.

ABI. No, it's like comparing apples to a garbage bag full of shit.

> *(She looks.)*

You can see like blood in the cement.

SHEILA. I'm not done yet!

And it's concrete.

Cement is an ingredient *in* concrete.

> *(She tries to re-smooth the concrete so no blood can be seen.)*

ABI. What is going on with you?

SHEILA. Nothing.

ABI. What happened with Tara Hutchinson?

> *(Beat.)*

C'mon, La-La, you never tell me anything anymore.

SHEILA. I tell you everything.

ABI. No, you don't.

SHEILA. Bee – I literally tell you everything that happens in my life.

ABI. Maybe you tell Derrick everything.

SHEILA. Derrick thinks I work in a call center.

A call center that has a lot of out-of-town assignments.

> *(She looks over the concrete and the general cleanliness of the kill area.)*

There.

So. Tara Hutchinson.

On my way here this morning, I saw her at the Shell. I hadn't seen her in forever.

She was filling up her minivan at the pump diagonal from me and she –

She was wearing the exact same jacket.

ABI. She was wearing a single-button chambray jacket from Zara?

SHEILA. Exactly the same.

ABI. Same color?

SHEILA. Yes.

So. She's clearly in a hurry – on her way to work – rushing to drop her two daughters off at school or daycare or whatever.

And they're in the back seat – braiding each other's hair – and they are so cute – like off-the-charts cute. These two little angels.

And I'm just staring and Tara hasn't seen me yet and when she turns,

I like jerk the other direction so she doesn't see me.

I don't want to talk to her. I don't want her asking me if I'm married and have a family. *Where I'm working.*

And when I look back, Tara's already getting back into the van – and the older girl suddenly pulls the younger one's braid. Like hard – like really, really hard. And the younger one screams "stop" so loud that everyone at the gas station turns and looks.

Then the older one like slap-scratches the younger one across the face – and Tara is yelling and the younger sister is crying and I –

I reach for my gun.

It takes everything in me *not* to draw it.

And I see it all. What I wish I could do:

I see myself drawing my Beretta

aiming

and shooting the older girl in the head – I see her face explode against the passenger-side window of the van –

ABI. Stop.

(Beat.)

SHEILA. And I would never do that.

> I don't think I would. But it's what I want to do. Dozens of times a day. Whenever someone wrongs someone else, I –
>
> ...I wish I could go through one day without thinking about killing.
>
> But it's...in my heart.
>
> It's what is in my heart.

ABI. Do you ever think about killing me?

SHEILA. No.

ABI. Do you? When I make you angry?

SHEILA. ...Yes.

> Don't you think about killing me?

ABI. No.

SHEILA. Really?

ABI. ...No.

SHEILA. Is it too late for me?

ABI. To what?

SHEILA. To stop. To get a nine-to-five job and a minivan.

ABI. You should talk to Mom.

SHEILA. I can't talk to her about this.

ABI. Maybe she could help – maybe she's gone through the same thing.

> We're different, La-La. I've never killed anyone.
>
> I've never listened to a person's last breaths.
>
> ...When you're out in the field, the crazier things get, the calmer you are.
>
> Sure, you may imagine all this morbid shit, but you don't do it.

SHEILA. *(Gesturing to the concrete grave.)* Um.

ABI. I mean, you don't do it outside of our business. You don't go killing people for free.

> But me on the other hand, I wouldn't trust myself to know where the line is.

When things get tense, I get belligerent.

It's why I'm good for the office and you're good for the field.

You should have heard me on the phone with Best Buy customer service. I was a monster. With a gun in my hands, I would have shot Becky from the Geek Squad in the face.

...Is everything okay with Derrick?

SHEILA. What? – yeah. Derrick and I are good.

ABI. But not great.

SHEILA. No, not great, but we're good. We're a solid good.

Derrick is the only man I've ever dated that...doesn't make me angry.

He's considerate. He's fun. He's moderately smart. He doesn't want to have sex too much.

ABI. And you don't want to kill him?

SHEILA. ...I don't.

ABI. That's good.

SHEILA. No, it's remarkable.

ABI. Yeah, I mean, you think about killing your own sister, but not your boyfriend – that's great.

I'm happy for you.

SHEILA. You'll find someone.

ABI. I know.

I totally will.

And he'll be awesome. He won't just be "good," he'll be awesome.

Right?

SHEILA. Right.

ABI. ...You're such a goober.

SHEILA. At least I'm not a freak.

ABI. Goober.

SHEILA. Freak.

ABI. Chicken butt.

SHEILA. Ass-face.

GLORIA. *(To* **SHEILA.***)* Who are you calling ass-face, shit-for-brains?

> *(***GLORIA*** enters.)*

ABI. Mom – how'd you not trip the sensors?

GLORIA. I jumped the sensors.

ABI. Why?

GLORIA. What is this? – no kisses from my girls?

ABI. Hi, Mom.

> *(She kisses* **GLORIA***'s cheek.)*

GLORIA. Hi, darling.

SHEILA. Hi, Mom.

> *(She kisses* **GLORIA***'s cheek.)*

GLORIA. Hi, shit-for-brains.

SHEILA. Why are you calling me shit-for-brains?

GLORIA. Why do you think?

SHEILA. Why are you two here?

GLORIA. We are here to make sure you have cleaned up this mess –

before we move on to your next mess.

Did you tell your sister what you did yet?

Did you tell her?

> *(Beat.)*

(To **ABI.***)* Todd McIntyre told shit-for-brains here that he has a half-sister.

ABI. He doesn't have a half-sister.

GLORIA. He claims he does.

SHEILA. How do you know that?

> *(***GLORIA*** gives* **SHEILA*** a look.)*

You bugged me?

GLORIA. *(To* **ABI.***)* And then he convinced shit-for-brains to write down the sister's number.

And then shit-for-brains *called* the number.

*(**ABI** gasps.)*

ABI. So you tell me everything, huh?

SHEILA. I hung up after the voicemail picked up.

> *(**GLORIA** draws her gun and puts it to **SHEILA**'s temple.)*

GLORIA. Hands up.

> *(Terrified, **SHEILA** puts her hands up.)*

> *(**GLORIA** un-holsters **SHEILA**'s gun and takes it.)*

ABI. What are you doing?

GLORIA. *(Calmly, to **SHEILA**.)* Get down on your knees.

> *(**SHEILA** gets down on her knees, her hands still up.)*

ABI. Mom –

GLORIA. *(To **ABI**.)* Zip it.
*(To **SHEILA**.)* Why did you call Todd's sister's phone number?

SHEILA. Our phones are untraceable.

GLORIA. Nothing is untraceable.
What were you going to say to her?

SHEILA. I don't know.

GLORIA. You have become a liability.

SHEILA. He wanted to talk to his sister. They'd left things on bad terms and he –

GLORIA. People will say anything in that position. You cannot listen.

SHEILA. All I could think about was Abi and how I would want that chance.

GLORIA. You have lost whatever made you great at this.
You want to take a pill to make it stop?
I will give you a pill.

> *(She takes the safety off her gun.)*

ABI. What is happening?

GLORIA. I have to do this. To protect you.

ABI. You're not thinking clearly.

GLORIA. On the contrary.

    Three.

SHEILA. I love you, Abi.

GLORIA. Two.

SHEILA.	**ABI**.
Get out of this / while you still can.	Jesus, Mom.

GLORIA. / One.

    *(***GLORIA*** pulls the trigger. ***ABI*** screams.)*

    (The gun clicks. It is not loaded.)

    (It takes a moment for ***SHEILA*** *to comprehend that she is still alive.)*

    (Perhaps she touches her head and looks at her hands.)

GLORIA. …Is your heart racing?

SHEILA. Yes.

GLORIA. Are you sweating?

SHEILA. Yes.

GLORIA. This is how it must be. Every day. Every project. As soon as you forget that any moment could be your last – then you are no longer the hunter.

You are the hunted.

You cannot second-guess yourself.

You cannot concern yourself with right and wrong.

There is only one question:

What is the job?

    (Beat.)

Abi, run the sister's number through the Tarnyx search. 726 –

SHEILA. Whoa, whoa, whoa – the job is not to kill the sister.

GLORIA. We need to gather intel on her – and then it's for the client to decide.

SHEILA. She didn't do anything.

GLORIA. If what Todd said is true, McIntyre Properties won't go to the state.

And that would be a size-large problem for our client.

SHEILA. I will have no part of this.

GLORIA. The only way we compete with the big dogs is that we guarantee our work.

We don't give you the runaround for two-and-a-half hours – we answer the call ourselves. We go the extra mile. We do it right.

That's what you get when you go local.

Run the number –

726-324-6644.

> (**ABI** *types in the phone number.*)

SHEILA. I can't do this anymore.

I'm done.

I am out.

> (*She starts to leave.*)

GLORIA. Give your holster to your sister. Before you go.

(To **ABI**, *showing her Sheila's gun.)* Abi, this is a nine-millimeter Beretta – one of the most reliable and deadly handguns in the world.

(Holding it out to her.) See how it feels in your hand.

> (**ABI** *holds up her hands and doesn't take it.*)

ABI. Agh, I hate guns.

SHEILA. What are you doing?

GLORIA. If you're going to leave us in the lurch, your little sister will have to pick up your slack.

SHEILA. Mom –

GLORIA. Don't "Mom" me, you made a goddamn mess and now you're gonna leave it to us to clean up? Get out of my sight. A desk job at a fucking non-profit awaits.

(To **ABI**.*)* The first rule of firearms:

Treat every weapon as though it is loaded. And this one is.

Take it.

Take it, Abigail.

> (**ABI** *takes the gun. She squirms with it in her hands.*)

ABI. La-La, please don't go.

> (*Beat.* **SHEILA** *comes back in and takes the gun from* **ABI.**)

SHEILA. I will help you finish this job and then that is it. For good.

> (*Beat.*)

GLORIA. (*To* **ABI.**) What do you got?

> (*Beat.*)

ABI. (*Reading from the laptop.*) The number belongs to Gabriella Sheridan.

Thirty years old. Six-foot-two. One hundred sixty-five pounds.

What is she – a WNBA player?

> (*She types.*)

Nope. She is a kindergarten teacher. Currently unemployed.

I don't see how they're related.

GLORIA. Well, let's pay her a visit and find out. What's her address?

ABI. (*Typing.*) It is...

Oh, shit! – oh shit, oh shit, oh shit.

GLORIA. What?

ABI. It's right across the street.

> (**GLORIA** *and* **SHEILA** *immediately drop to the floor.*)

> (*Off their lead,* **ABI** *awkwardly crouches, still typing on the laptop.*)

(**GLORIA** *and* **SHEILA** *grab the gear that Abi brought and, staying low to the ground, make their way to the wall.*)

(**SHEILA** *gets out the binoculars.*)

SHEILA. What apartment?

ABI. 3C.

(**SHEILA** *pulls aside the plastic and looks outside with the binoculars.*)

SHEILA. Which way does it face?

ABI. Working on it.

GLORIA. Get into that building's security system.

ABI. Working on it.

(**SHEILA** *returns to lying low.*)

SHEILA. Doesn't look like anyone is home on the whole third floor.

Are you in yet?

ABI. Not yet.

SHEILA. What is taking so long?

ABI. Hacking into an Amcrest 960H Security System takes more than four seconds.

SHEILA. You've had more than four seconds.

ABI. I'm going as fast as I can, chicken butt.

SHEILA. Well, go faster, ass-face.

(*Beat.*)

(**SHEILA** *checks to make sure her Beretta is loaded. It is.*)

(**GLORIA** *drops the empty clip from her gun. She puts in a new clip.*)

(**GLORIA** *and* **SHEILA**, *at the same time, lock and load their Berettas.*)

GLORIA. Isn't this nice? The three of us in the field together for the first time.

(*She reaches out and squeezes both* **SHEILA** *and* **ABI**.)

GLORIA. I can't think of a better way for us to spend Sheila's last day.

(Blackout.)

(Seven hours later.)

(Dusk.)

*(**GLORIA**, **SHEILA**, and **ABI** lie close to the floor.)*

*(**GLORIA** has a camera with a telephoto lens.)*

*(**SHEILA** holds binoculars.)*

*(**ABI** periodically checks the surveillance feeds on her laptop.)*

(There are three empty Chipotle fountain drink cups around them. The rest of the trash from their lunch is in the Chipotle bag.)

SHEILA. Anything?

ABI. *(Looking at the computer.)* Nothing yet.

(They wait.)

SHEILA. *(Quietly singing.)*
She'll be comin' round the mountain when she comes –

(She kneels, pulls back the plastic, and looks outside with binoculars.)

(She methodically searches.)

She'll be comin' round the mountain when she comes
She'll be comin' round the mountain
She'll be comin' round the mountain –
She'll be comin' round the mountain when she comes.
She'll be drivin' six white horses when she comes
She'll be drivin' six white horses when she comes –

GLORIA. Will you shut the fuck up?

*(**SHEILA** returns to lying low.)*

SHEILA. All clear.
Where the hell is she?

GLORIA. Not home yet.

SHEILA. Maybe she's on vacation.

ABI. She bought a cinnamon sugar bagel with jalapeño cream cheese at Einstein's this morning. She's not on vacation.

SHEILA. That is the worst bagel cream cheese combo I have ever heard of.

ABI. There's no one home in any of these apartments. This neighborhood is the worst.

SHEILA. And all of these buildings are owned by McIntyre Properties?

ABI. Yes.

> (**GLORIA** *kneels, puts her camera through the plastic, and scans the building across the street.*)

SHEILA. You've checked all the deeds?

ABI. Checked and double-checked.

SHEILA. Air space?

ABI. Everything.

> (**GLORIA** *returns to lying low.*)

GLORIA. Still no activity on the cell number?

ABI. Nada. There's a good chance she doesn't know Todd passed away yet.

SHEILA. I don't know if what happened to Todd qualifies as passing away.

ABI. There's a good chance the sister doesn't know her brother was shot in the head by an assassin and then buried in cement.

> (**SHEILA** *raises her finger.*)

Concrete.

SHEILA. Are you sure you've hacked into all of the security cameras on this block?

ABI. Um, yes.

SHEILA. You don't have to get so defensive about it.

ABI. We are *here* because of *your* screwup.

GLORIA. You haven't found anything more about the will or the trust?

ABI. No. His father's will said everything was split between his wife – who died at the same time – and Todd. Pending what is stated in the trust.

But the trust is not public record and I haven't been able to hack into his attorney's database because – as far as I can tell – they don't have one.

SHEILA. Who doesn't have a database?

ABI. Those who want to do business with the utmost discretion.

And old people.

> *(Beat.)*

It's been seven hours. How much longer are we gonna wait here?

GLORIA. As long as it takes to gather the intel we need.

ABI. I'm starving.

I have a bag of chips, but I'm saving them. Until I can't not eat them.

> *(Beat.)*

Cheddar and Sour Cream Baked Lays.

> *(Beat.)*

The whole bag is only 130 calories and four grams of fat.

> *(Beat.)*

I need to pee.

GLORIA. Then use the bucket. It's not good to hold it.

ABI. Cover me.

> *(She commandos over to the bucket.)*
>
> *(Perhaps GLORIA and SHEILA roll their eyes at her.)*
>
> *(After ABI gets across the room, GLORIA speaks.)*

GLORIA. You know what my longest stakeout was?

SHEILA, ABI & GLORIA. "A hundred-and-twenty-six hours."

SHEILA & ABI. "I didn't eat, I hardly even blinked, I peed in a cup."

GLORIA. Okay, okay, okay –

SHEILA. "It was a different time. It was –"

GLORIA. So I've told you the story, but the moral is: Seven hours is nothing.

> *(The sound of* ABI *peeing into a five-gallon bucket.)*

> *(*GLORIA *and* SHEILA *listen.)*

SHEILA. I really, really, really need to pee.

GLORIA. Use the bucket after your sister.

SHEILA. That is so gross.

GLORIA. It's not so bad, is it, Abi?

ABI. *(Still unseen.)* I mean, I wish we had toilet paper.

GLORIA. Use the bucket, Sheila. It's better than peeing in your pants.

ABI. This bucket is filthy.

GLORIA. *(To* ABI.*)* Well, don't sit on it!

> *(The sound of* ABI *peeing from a greater height. They listen.)*

(To SHEILA.*)* You just have to go number one, right?

SHEILA. Yeah, but I'm just getting over this UTI and –

GLORIA. Another one? You need to stop wearing those tight yoga pants all the time.

SHEILA. Mom.

GLORIA. You pee after you and Derrick ee-un ee-un, right?

SHEILA. Yes, Mom.

GLORIA. Well then, I don't think Dr. Molli is giving you the right antibiotics if you keep getting them.

SHEILA. Can we please talk about something else so I don't keep thinking about how bad I have to pee?

GLORIA. It's not good for you to hold it.

SHEILA. Mom.

> *(*ABI *commandos back.)*

> *(She takes Purell out of one of the gear bags and uses it.)*

ABI. I didn't know "She'll be drivin' six white horses" was the next verse.

And what's after that?

SHEILA. *(Speaking the lyrics, matter-of-factly.)* She'll be wearin' pink pajamas when she comes.

Then – Oh, we'll all come out to meet her when she comes.

She'll be carryin' three white puppies when she comes.

We will kill the old red rooster when she comes.

We will all have chicken and dumplin's when she comes.

ABI. You're making this up.

SHEILA. Those are the lyrics.

> *(She looks something up on her phone.)*
>
> *(They wait.)*
>
> *(**GLORIA** sees **SHEILA** on her phone.)*

GLORIA. What are you doing?

SHEILA. Nothing.

GLORIA. That better be work email.

SHEILA. Crap, I need to check that, too.

GLORIA. Put it away.

SHEILA. Mom –

GLORIA. Phones away!

You are always on that damn thing. Whether you're playing Bedazzled or –

SHEILA. Bejeweled.

GLORIA. Be-who-the-fuck-cares. This situation doesn't command your full attention?

SHEILA. I'm sorry, okay?

GLORIA. You're like the people with courtside seats checking their phones during the match. Really? Is that really more interesting than Serena Williams playing tennis ten feet away from you?

SHEILA. I look at it all the time. I can multitask. I grew up multitasking.

GLORIA. Oh, and I didn't? After your father was shot in the head –

SHEILA & ABI. God rest his soul.

GLORIA. I had to run the business myself and raise two girls. You don't think you have to multitask for that?

> *(ABI tries to discreetly check something on her phone.)*

SHEILA. I just mean – quickly checking my phone doesn't screw up my focus. Like it does for you.

GLORIA. Abi, could you please tell your sister to –

> *(She sees ABI on her phone.)*

Oh, for crying out loud!

What is so important? Both of you? What can't wait?

SHEILA. Nothing.

ABI. Nothing.

GLORIA. Nothing can wait. What was it?

SHEILA. I was just looking up the origin of "She'll be Comin' 'Round the Mountain."

GLORIA. Why didn't you ask me? Why would you Google before you ask the human beings around you?

ABI. What is it?

GLORIA. It's a children's version of an old spiritual called "When the Chariot Comes."

ABI. So who's the "she" – in she'll be comin' around the mountain?

GLORIA. The she is the chariot that Jesus is comin' round the mountain in. For the Second Coming.

SHEILA. Wikipedia said it's for the End of Days.

> *(She holds up her phone to show GLORIA.)*

GLORIA. No more screens!

ABI. I need the laptop for the security feed!

GLORIA. No more phones! Put 'em away or I will throw them out the godforsaken window.

Or where there should be a window.

> *(ABI and SHEILA put away their phones.)*

> *(To ABI.)* And what were you looking up, missy?

ABI. I got a Snapchat.

GLORIA. Here lies my dear beloved daughter, Abigail. She needed to check her Snapchat and while she did, she got shot in the head. May she rest in peace.

SHEILA. We're sorry we checked our phones, okay?

GLORIA. Sorry doesn't cut it. This is a life-and-death situation and if I see either of you motherfucking Snapchatting –

SHEILA. I don't Snapchat.

GLORIA. You two need to stop clowning around and *focus.* We are flying in the dark on this because of shit-for-brains here. So get your mother-lovin' heads in the game. *Now.*

> *(She looks through the camera and focuses the telephoto lens.)*
>
> (**SHEILA** *looks through the binoculars.)*
>
> (**ABI** *looks at the video feeds on the laptop.)*

I mean, seven hours is nothing.

> *(They wait.)*

Your generation and these phones...
Your minds have gone to mush.

> *(They wait.)*

You don't know how to be alone with your own thoughts.

> *(They wait.)*

You've got no endurance.

> *(They wait.)*

None. Zero. Zilch.

> *(They wait.)*

Seven hours – give me a break.

> *(They wait.)*

Break me off a piece of that Kit-Kat bar.

> *(They wait.)*

GLORIA. You know, frankly, it's sad.

You are all soft and it's sad.

Feel my wrist.

(She holds out her wrist.)

C'mon, Abi. Feel it.

*(**ABI** feels **GLORIA***'s wrist.)*

What do you feel? Hm?

I am cold-blooded.

ABI. Feels warm to me.

GLORIA. It's cold.

Feel it, Sheila.

SHEILA. Mom –

GLORIA. C'mon! – feel it.

*(**SHEILA** feels **GLORIA***'s wrist.)*

What do you feel?

SHEILA. I feel ice running through your veins.

GLORIA. Exactly.

I have it. You have it.

And we –

ABI. What about me?

GLORIA. What about you?

ABI. Do I have ice running through my veins?

GLORIA. Do you think you do?

ABI. ...No.

GLORIA. No, Abigail, what you have – are your father's brains and his bad eyesight.

(Beat.)

Anything else from the Tarnyx search about this six-foot-two, hundred-and-sixty-five-pound Amazon sister?

ABI. Nope.

GLORIA. I want to know as soon as the sister buys anything, uses her cell phone, or comes anywhere near here.

ABI. I promise to let you know, ma'am.

GLORIA. Don't call me ma'am.

ABI. Can we order Jimmy John's or something?

SHEILA. We can't order out twice in one day – that's the rule.

ABI. I think we can make an exception today.

Besides, I did like an hour of bat-out-of-hell elliptical last night.

GLORIA. *(Suddenly emotional.)* We're not ordering motherfucking Jimmy John.

> *(She cries. A few moments pass.)*

ABI. It's Jimmy John's.

With an s.

> **(GLORIA** *weeps.)*

GLORIA. Oh, God –

> **(ABI** *and* **SHEILA** *let her weep.)*
>
> *(After a few moments,* **ABI** *takes out her small bag of Baked Lays. She opens it. It's noisy.* **GLORIA** *glares at her.* **ABI** *doesn't notice.)*
>
> **(ABI** *eats a chip. She chews loudly. She eats another.)*
>
> **(GLORIA** *grabs the bag of chips and slowly does a death grip on it.)*

ABI. Oh, come on, Mom.

> **(GLORIA** *thoroughly crushes the chips.)*

Really?

GLORIA. Focus.

> **(ABI** *picks up the bag. She pours the smashed pieces of chips into her hand and tries to eat them. The pieces go everywhere.)*

Pick those up.

ABI. This is an abandoned construction site. No one cares if –

GLORIA. The birds will start coming.

ABI. Birds don't come in here.

GLORIA. Where do you think all the bird shit over there came from?

    (The squawk of a crow nearby.)

Pick them up. Both of you. We can't have a murder of crows coming in here.

SHEILA. I didn't do it.

GLORIA. Help your sister. The birds could give away our location.

ABI. Never once have I thought: "Look at that flock of birds on that building under construction. There must be a family of assassins staked out in there."

GLORIA. No, but you *look* at the birds. And we don't want anyone *looking* where we are for any reason.

    (Another squawk.)

For crying out loud.

    (She starts picking up the tiny pieces of chips.)

    *(After a few moments, **SHEILA** starts picking up the chips as well.)*

    *(Reluctantly, **ABI** starts to help.)*

No, Abi – we've got it.

ABI. I can't believe you smashed the only food I have.

GLORIA. I can't believe you dumped chips all over the place.

ABI. When we're done with this, you're totally taking us to Olive Garden.

SHEILA. We are not going to Olive Garden.

ABI. I love Olive Garden and the people that diss it are nothing but uppity bitches.

    (Pause.)

GLORIA. So what else would you do?

So what else would you do?
What would you actually do – if not this?

SHEILA. I don't know. I feel totally unqualified to do anything else.

GLORIA. You want out so bad, what's your plan?

SHEILA. I don't have a plan.

GLORIA. There must be something else you want to do.

SHEILA. ...I want to be a mom.

GLORIA. You can do both.

(**SHEILA** *laughs.*)

What is funny about that? I did both.

SHEILA. Mom.

GLORIA. I'm doing both.

SHEILA. The thought of bringing a life into this world – while I'm still taking lives out of it –
I couldn't.

GLORIA. Did you just call me a hypocrite?

SHEILA. No.

GLORIA. Then you just called me a bad mother.

SHEILA. No, but you are a mother who made it clear to her children that her work came first.

(**GLORIA** *looks the other way, deeply stung – but* **SHEILA** *continues.*)

And maybe if you'd been around a little more, Abi and I wouldn't have turned out like this.

ABI. What's wrong with us?

SHEILA. Um, we're killers.

ABI. I don't pull the trigger.

SHEILA. You pull the trigger by association.

ABI. So I suppose you think the president is a killer, then.

SHEILA. The president *is* a killer.

GLORIA. That's enough of this talk – Silent Time.

SHEILA. You don't get to call Silent Time anymore.

GLORIA. Well, I just did so Snapchat that. Silence in three, two, one.

(*They are silent. They wait.*)

(*A long time passes.*)

(Eventually, unable to keep this in –)

GLORIA. *(To* **SHEILA.***)* You can be good at this job and good at being a mother, you ungrateful little shit.

> *(This hangs in the air.)*
>
> *(They wait.)*
>
> *(They wait.)*

I did *everything* in my power to keep this from you.

My mother had me firing an M14 before I could ride a bike.

I was determined not to force it on you like she forced it on me.

So I kept it from you two – and I kept it from your father.

SHEILA & ABI. God rest his soul.

SHEILA. You would've just kept it from all of us?

GLORIA. Absolutely.

SHEILA. You would've let us go on thinking you were an emergency spill responder for the E.P.A.?

> *(***GLORIA*** smiles.)*

Daddy must have suspected something.

GLORIA. Sure, he did. But he respected that I had some doors I wouldn't open for him.

And goddammit, I loved him for it.

There's not a day goes by I don't wish Gilbert Kolinski blew off my head instead – not a day I don't wish you two followed in your daddy's footsteps instead of mine.

But no – *you* had to look

you had to start asking questions

you had to take matters into your own hands.

SHEILA. I was fifteen years old. You should have stopped me.

GLORIA. You couldn't be stopped. You shot Gilbert Kolinski in the head and cut out his heart – all on your own – and I –

> *(The laptop beeps.)*

ABI. Someone just triggered the sensor on the west stairwell.

SHEILA. In her condo?

ABI. No, in this building.

GLORIA & SHEILA. Shit.

> (**GLORIA** *and* **SHEILA** *quickly put away the gear.*)

SHEILA. Who's got lead?

GLORIA. I'll take it.

SHEILA. Keep the laptop out. Make it a part of the presentation.

ABI. Tripped it on the second floor.

GLORIA. Jackets.

> (**GLORIA** *and* **SHEILA** *put on their suit jackets to cover their guns.*)

ABI. Third floor.

GLORIA. *(With a complete shift in her demeanor.)* So ladies, if you think you have the equity to take a risk like this –

> (**AMI** *enters from the stairwell. She is seventeen, short, and thin. She wears a purple backpack. She watches* **ABI**, **SHEILA**, *and* **GLORIA** *for a few moments.*)

SHEILA. Just level with us. Why did McIntyre Properties shut down construction? Is the area too flooded with vacant commercial space?

GLORIA. No. They filed for Chapter 7 bankruptcy.

SHEILA. But do you know why? Before we invest in this property, we –

GLORIA. Oh, excuse us. Hello.

AMI. Hello.

GLORIA. Can we help you?

AMI. Can you?

GLORIA. Well, do you have an extra thirty-five million dollars? These broads are dragging their feet.

SHEILA. I wouldn't call it dragging –

GLORIA. This is the third time you've asked to tour the property.

ABI. Sorry, but this is a closed site. You can't be here.

AMI. I come here every day after school.

ABI. It's almost eight o'clock.

AMI. I had scholastic bowl practice today. I just come in here to smoke.

ABI. Smoking will kill you.

SHEILA. *(To* **ABI.***)* Cynthia, where are your manners?

ABI. What the hell is scholastic bowl?

AMI. It's like *Jeopardy!* but with teams.

SHEILA. We're considering buying this property. Do you live around here?

AMI. This is on my way home.

SHEILA. How do you like the neighborhood?

AMI. It sucks.

Everything went out of business after the Super Target opened.

GLORIA. Well, young lady, I'm the exclusive agent for this property and I'm afraid –

AMI. I thought Ms. Baxter was.

GLORIA. Oh, Ms. Baxter sold out and went over to Re/Max last week. It's a ruthless business – real estate. Headhunters left and right.

But I'm afraid we can't have you in here, dear. Insurance mandates it.

AMI. What about them?

ABI. We signed disclaimers, duh.

AMI. I can sign one.

I dream of going into real estate. I wanna go into a ruthless business with headhunters left and right.

I think it's so pretty up here, don't you? How unfinished it is.

(The laptop beeps. **ABI** *checks it.)*

ABI. We have to keep moving. Time is money. Time is money. Whaddya say, time is money.

> (**GLORIA** *and* **SHEILA** *look at* **ABI** *as if to say, "Get a grip."*)

GLORIA. Let me walk you out, young lady.

AMI. That's okay. I know this place backwards and forwards. If you ever want an intern or something – just let me know. I'll probably be smoking up here after scholastic bowl practice if you ever want to find me.

> (*She leaves.*)

ABI. *(Whispering.)* The security system was just disengaged at the sister's apartment.

> (*She quickly takes out the camera with the telephoto lens.*)

GLORIA. Hold on – wait until the girl is out of the building.

ABI. We can't wait!

SHEILA. Get a grip, Abi.

GLORIA. What's on the video?

ABI. Nothing yet.

> (**SHEILA** *takes out the binoculars.*)

SHEILA. Was the security system disengaged onsite or remotely?

AMI. What are you doing?

> (**GLORIA, SHEILA,** *and* **ABI** *spin around.* **AMI** *has just walked back in.*)

ABI. None of your beeswax!

AMI. I just remembered I have some resumes in my backpack. I wanted to give you one.

ABI. Get down on the ground!

AMI. What?

SHEILA. Cynthia, what are you –

ABI. Or you'll wind up at the bottom of the river!

> (**AMI** *gets down on the ground.*)

SHEILA. You don't need to get down on the ground.

> (**AMI** *starts to get up.*)

ABI. Stay down, half-pint!

> (**AMI** *gets back down.*)

SHEILA. *(To* **ABI.***)* Zip it.
(To **AMI.***)* You get her out of the office for one day and all of a sudden she thinks she's Bruce Willis.

GLORIA. Let us help you up off this filthy floor.

> (**GLORIA** *and* **SHEILA** *help* **AMI** *up.*)

We'll take that resume and then we won't take up any more of your time.

> (**AMI** *takes off her backpack.*)

ABI. Slower! What's in the book bag, half-pint?

AMI. Resumes.

ABI. Liar!

AMI. We had to make them for Career Day.

> (*The computer beeps again.*)

ABI. It says there's movement in the apartment.

> (*She points out toward the apartment across the street.*)

There she is!

> (*For a moment,* **GLORIA, SHEILA,** *and* **ABI** *look out toward the apartment.*)

> (**AMI** *reaches into her backpack and takes out a .32 caliber revolver.*)

> (**AMI** *goes up to* **ABI.** **ABI** *turns. For a moment,* **ABI** *looks at* **AMI** *and the gun, confused.*)

> (**AMI** *shoots* **ABI** *in the head.*)

> (*A mess from* **ABI***'s head splatters all over* **GLORIA***'s blouse.*)

> (**ABI** *falls over in a heap.*)

*(As **GLORIA** turns, **AMI** hits her across the face with the butt of the revolver.)*

*(**GLORIA** falls over, unconscious.)*

*(**AMI** aims the gun at **SHEILA**.)*

*(**SHEILA** reaches for her Beretta.)*

AMI. Hands up!

Now!

*(**SHEILA** holds up her hands and freezes.)*

*(**AMI** starts shaking as she aims the gun at **SHEILA**.)*

SHEILA. Put it down.

*(She steps closer to **AMI**.)*

Put that down and let me help my sister.

AMI. You can't help her. Just like I can't help Todd.

SHEILA. …You're her?

You're the sister. But you're not –

AMI. I am not six-foot-two. I'm not thirty years old. I'm not a hundred and sixty-five pounds. Who hired you?

*(**SHEILA** reaches for her gun.)*

Don't!

*(She fires a warning shot over **SHEILA**'s head. **SHEILA** freezes.)*

I don't want to kill you.

SHEILA. Then don't.

AMI. I needed you to feel what I feel. A sister for a brother. It's up to you if the killing stops here.

(Blackout.)

End of Act One

ACT TWO

(Later that night. Around two a.m.)

*(**GLORIA** and **SHEILA** are tied to chairs – about ten feet apart from one another.)*

(They are sweating, out of breath. They are trying to scoot their chairs toward the pile of construction equipment in the corner. However, they are tied so tightly to their chairs they are barely moving.)

(There is a new patch of wet concrete in the section of unfinished floor. It is messy and uneven.)

(Ami is gone.)

GLORIA. Color?

(Beat.)

SHEILA. Purple.

GLORIA. Purple.

(They try to scoot.)

SHEILA. Number?

(Beat.)

GLORIA & SHEILA. Three.

(They try to scoot.)

GLORIA. Movie?

(Beat.)

GLORIA & SHEILA. *The Princess Bride.*

(They try to scoot.)

GLORIA. Second-favorite movie?

Amélie.

SHEILA. No, *Labyrinth.*

GLORIA. She watched *Amélie* a hundred times when she had mono.

SHEILA. She wanted to marry David Bowie.

(*They try to scoot.*)

Lettuce?

GLORIA. What?

SHEILA. What was Abi's favorite lettuce?

(*Beat.*)

Romaine.

GLORIA. Kale.

SHEILA. Kale isn't lettuce.

GLORIA. Sure, it is.

SHEILA. Kale is a vegetable, but it's not lettuce.

GLORIA. Well, she liked kale way more than romaine – that's all I'm saying.

(*They scoot.*)

Book?

(*Beat.*)

Jane Eyre.

SHEILA. *Jane Eyre* was not her favorite book.

GLORIA. Sure, it was.

SHEILA. Her favorite book was *Ms. Quarterback.*

GLORIA. What is *Ms. Quarterback*?

SHEILA. It's a *Sweet Valley High* book. Number seventy.

GLORIA. That is not her favorite book.

SHEILA. She literally told me it was her favorite book.

GLORIA. What's it about?

SHEILA. I'll give you one guess.

I can't keep going through Abi's favorites – it's making me too sad.

This is all my fault.

GLORIA. No, this is on me. I knew you were slipping, but I looked the other way.

I wanted to use the ol' fake execution trick on you last weekend, but I chickened out.

SHEILA. I am a *professional*. How did I let this happen?

GLORIA. We all screwed up.

SHEILA. *(Yelling as long and as loud as she can.)* Fuuuuuck!

> *(There is a slight echo through the abandoned building.)*

Siri?

Siri?

Siri!

GLORIA. She took our phones.

SHEILA. Guns?

GLORIA. Took 'em.

SHEILA. Laptop?

GLORIA. Took it.

SHEILA. *And* the hacksaw?

GLORIA. *Gone.*

SHEILA. That was my favorite hacksaw.

GLORIA. We'll get you another hacksaw, dear.

SHEILA. That was the one I used on Gilbert Kolinski.

> *(Beat.)*

Did that little bitch really bury Abi in the concrete next to Todd?

GLORIA. Try not to think about it.

> *(She tries to scoot. **SHEILA** doesn't.)*

SHEILA. I have to pee so bad.

GLORIA. Should've gone in the bucket.

SHEILA. And trying to scoot this chair is really not helping. I have never had to pee so bad in my entire life.

GLORIA. Don't think about it – only think about getting to the tools in the corner. There's gotta be something we can use to cut these ropes.

SHEILA. The only reason the girl found us is because I called that stupid number.

GLORIA. Don't look back, look forward.

Animal.

SHEILA. Why didn't she kill us?

GLORIA. C'mon. Favorite animal.

SHEILA. Why did she tie us up and leave us? Is she coming back?

GLORIA. Horses!

Oh, Abi drew the most beautiful horses when she was a girl.

SHEILA. If she wants to know who our client is – why isn't she here torturing us?

GLORIA. Focus on making it to the corner.

We will find an X-Acto knife.

We will cut ourselves free.

> *(The muffled sound of a cell phone ringing. It is barely audible.)*
>
> *(The ring is a hip-hop or pop song.*)*
>
> (**GLORIA** *and* **SHEILA** *look around.)*

SHEILA. That's my phone – that's Derrick's ring.

Where is it?

Siri! Answer! Answer call!

Where is it...

GLORIA. It sounds like it's buried in the cement.

---

*A license to produce *Kill Local* does not include a performance license for any third-party or copyrighted music. Licensees should create an original composition or use music in the public domain. For further information, please see Music Use Note on page 3.

SHEILA. Siri, answer!

GLORIA. Siri, answer!

> *(The ringing stops.)*

SHEILA. Answer, Siri!

GLORIA. Answer!

SHEILA. Why would she leave it on?

GLORIA. Rookie mistake?

SHEILA. I can't believe we let a rookie do this to us.

GLORIA. Don't look back, look forward.

SHEILA. Abi knew something was off with that girl.

GLORIA. Right now we need a big scoot for Abi on three. One. Two. Three.

> *(She tries to scoot.* **SHEILA** *does not.)*

C'mon, Sheila – scoot! You'd never believe the terrible situations I've gotten myself out of with the power of positive thinking.

SHEILA. With positive thinking?

GLORIA. That's right.

SHEILA. You want some positive thinking?

GLORIA. I do.

Big push on three.

GLORIA & SHEILA. One – two – three!

> *(They jerk their bodies as hard as they can, but their chairs still don't move.* **SHEILA** *pees herself.)*

SHEILA. Mom? I had an accident.

> *(A puddle of urine forms on the floor.)*

GLORIA. It's okay, dear.

SHEILA. I am so sorry.

GLORIA. It's okay.

SHEILA. I am so, so sorry.

GLORIA. Hey, hey, hey – shh. Shh, baby girl.

SHEILA. I can't believe Abi's gone.

GLORIA. We will mourn later, okay?

Shh.

Okay?

SHEILA. *(Quietly.)* If I didn't pick the lock and open the casket –

if I never saw Daddy's face blown apart –

GLORIA. God rest his soul.

SHEILA. – where would I be right now?

Who would I be?

Would I be a Tara Hutchinson?

GLORIA. Do you want to be a Tara Hutchinson?

SHEILA. I wouldn't mind trading places with her right about now.

GLORIA. So what's the dream here?

You and Derrick get a labradoodle.

You work nine to five and throw pool party barbecues on the weekend?

SHEILA. Sounds good to me.

GLORIA. You wouldn't last a week at a desk job.

SHEILA. Yes, I would.

GLORIA. And what about kids?

How many?

SHEILA. ...Two.

Three.

GLORIA. Three?

You know how hard it is for normal people *not* to kill their children?

For us, it's a whole 'nother battle.

I mean, it was a *daily* struggle for me.

Still is.

(Beat.)

SHEILA. Why did you lock the casket?

GLORIA. For heaven's sake, Sheila, let it go.

SHEILA. Who locks a casket?

GLORIA. Who picks the lock of a locked casket?

SHEILA. I needed to say goodbye.

GLORIA. Where did you even learn how to pick a lock?

SHEILA. Daddy taught me.

GLORIA. He did not.

SHEILA. Yes, he did.

He told me not to tell you.

GLORIA. Then why are you telling me now?

SHEILA. Because.

(Beat.)

If we get free – how do I not kill this girl?

(Beat.)

How did you not kill Gilbert Kolinski?

GLORIA. Because Gilbert Kolinski wasn't the job.

I kill for money.

I don't kill for right or wrong. Or for revenge.

This is my job. I excel at it. And I excel at it because I don't make it personal.

SHEILA. But he killed your husband – how could you let him live?

GLORIA. Did killing him bring your daddy back?

Did it?

I had no interest in killing Gilbert Kolinski because there wasn't anything in the world that was gonna bring back my man.

Killing only leads to more killing.

If you are serious about stopping, you cannot say after one more – you have to stop now. You have to kill the thing within you that needs to do this – right now.

SHEILA. ...Do *you* want to kill this girl?

GLORIA. ...Only if the client makes her part of the job.

Nothing will bring back my daughter.

...And if you want some small shred of good to come from Abi's death –

let it be the thing that makes you stop.

Here. And now.

If you ever see that girl again, look her in the eye and say, "We're even."

(She closes her eyes and lowers her head.)

Forgive us our trespasses as we forgive those who trespass against us.

*(**SHEILA** closes her eyes.)*

SHEILA. Forgive us our trespasses as we forgive those who trespass against us.

SHEILA & GLORIA. Forgive us our trespasses as we forgive those who trespass against us.

GLORIA. How does that feel? In your heart?

SHEILA. I don't know.

(Blackout.)

(The next afternoon. It is bright outside.)

*(**AMI** sits up on the scaffolding in the corner.)*

(There are numerous five-gallon buckets up on the scaffolding.)

*(In one hand, **AMI** holds a McCafé coffee cup.)*

(In her other hand, she holds a nearly finished cigarette.)

(The smoke swirls above her.)

*(**GLORIA** is asleep. She hasn't moved far. There is a puddle of urine underneath her chair.)*

*(**SHEILA** is asleep in the corner. Her chair is tipped over on its side, but she is still firmly tied to it. The construction materials are a mess – as though **SHEILA** tried everything to get free and nothing worked.)*

*(**AMI** puts out the cigarette.)*

*(A gust of wind blows through the building. The plastic sheets over where there should be windows breathe in and out with the wind. It is a strange, haunting sound. **AMI** listens. She sips her coffee.)*

(She times her breathing to line up with the in and out of the wind.)

(She breathes in.)

(She breathes out.)

(A loose piece of plastic flaps quietly.)

(She breathes in.)

(Blackout.)

(A couple of hours later. The sun is setting.)

*(**GLORIA** and **SHEILA** are awake. They've moved a couple of feet.)*

*(**AMI** is nowhere to be seen.)*

*(**GLORIA** is upright in her chair. **SHEILA** is still on the floor on her side.)*

(They are exhausted. They are soiled.)

(They are still firmly tied to their chairs.)

*(**GLORIA** hums Morse code on a single pitch.)*

(Note: she just hums the dots and dashes. She does not speak the letters.)

GLORIA.

. .	I
. – . .	L
– – –	O
. . . –	V
.	E
– . – –	Y
– – –	O
. . –	U

SHEILA. ...I love you too, Mom.

*(They wait in silence. Then **SHEILA** hums.)*

. . .	S
– – –	O
. . .	S

GLORIA.

. . .	S
– – –	O
. . .	S

SHEILA & GLORIA.

. . .	S
– – –	O

...   S

(They do it again, in harmony.)

...   S
– – –   O
...   S

(They do it again, louder.)

...   S
– – –   O
...   S

SHEILA. You think anyone understands S.O.S. in Morse code anymore?

GLORIA. Nope!

SHEILA & GLORIA. *(Loudly.)*

...   S
– – –   O
...   S

(They laugh.)

SHEILA. *(Yelling.)* Help!

GLORIA. Help!

SHEILA. Help us!

(They laugh.)

GLORIA. I haven't heard a car go by in hours.

SHEILA. Somebody help us!

(The setting sun is low in the horizon. The light makes long shadows across the floor.)

GLORIA. Look at how the light is hitting the wall there. Almost looks...what color would you call that?

SHEILA. ...Amber.

GLORIA. Almost looks amber, doesn't it?

(They look.)

(A couple of crows squawk outside.)

(The sound of their wings flapping.)

SHEILA. "Look at those crows on that building under construction. There must be a family of assassins in there."

(They laugh.)

It's been about twenty-four hours we've been tied up.

GLORIA. Scoot on three.

One, two, three.

(They both, very meekly, try to scoot. They don't go anywhere.)

(They wait in silence.)

SHEILA. ...Are we going to die?

GLORIA. ...It's not looking good.

We really should stop clowning around and save our strength.

SHEILA. For what?

GLORIA. For whatever comes next.

(Pause.)

SHEILA. Boo!

GLORIA. Booga booga boo!

(They laugh.)

(Blackout.)

(A couple of hours later. It is around ten or eleven p.m.)

(SHEILA and GLORIA are asleep in their chairs. Again, they are in slightly different positions.)

(AMI carefully peeks her head through the stairwell door.)

(She slowly enters.)

(She holds a McCafé cup. Steam rises from it.)

(She wears her backpack.)

(She takes out the hacksaw.)

(She sits down on a five-gallon bucket a few feet away from SHEILA.)

(After watching SHEILA for a few moments, AMI nudges her with the handle of the hacksaw.)

AMI. *(Quietly.)* Hey.

Hey.

Hey.

(SHEILA stirs.)

Hey.

(SHEILA opens her eyes. She stares at AMI.)

(SHEILA breathes in like she's going to call out for GLORIA.)

Before you wake up your mother, can I talk to just you?

SHEILA. *(Quietly.)* Why just me?

AMI. Because you scare me less.

(GLORIA wakes up. She opens her eyes.)

(SHEILA and GLORIA look at one another.)

(AMI doesn't notice GLORIA.)

(GLORIA closes her eyes and pretends to keep sleeping.)

How did you get upright again?

SHEILA. I knew a lifetime of jiu-jitsu, Pilates, and yoga would come in handy one day.

>   *(Beat.)*

Namaste.

>   *(Beat.)*

How'd you know I fell over?

AMI. I came to check on you earlier.

SHEILA. To see if the crows were pecking out our eyes yet?

>   *(Beat.)*

You didn't bring me a latte?

AMI. No.

SHEILA. *(A judgment.)* A McCafé.

AMI. It's the only place around open twenty-four hours.

SHEILA. Can I have a sip?

AMI. No.

SHEILA. I would kill for some coffee right now.

AMI. I thought you wanted to stop killing.

SHEILA. You have us bugged?

AMI. Sort of.

SHEILA. What does that mean?

AMI. Who hired you?

SHEILA. I don't know, only my mom knows. Shall we wake her up?

AMI. Not yet.

...Do you understand what you did?

Do you understand that Todd was the last person I had left in the whole world?

SHEILA. Then why didn't you kill me? My sister didn't do anything to you.

AMI. I already told you.

SHEILA. You needed me to feel what you feel.

How Old Testament of you.

AMI. But what I didn't think about was –

is –

is how *I* would feel.

I... I've had a really shitty life and every time I think it's gotten as shitty as it can possibly get, there's always a new level of shitty-ness.

After I realized you killed Todd, I didn't think I could feel any worse.

But since killing your sister, I feel worse.

And I was just gonna leave you two here, I was gonna never look back,

but that'd pretty much mean I'd be killing you two as well – so then it'd be up to three. And I don't want to be up to three.

A sister for a brother? That's an eye for an eye.

But a sister and her sister and their mother – for a brother?

That's something else.

That's a disproportionate response. And it would suck to have that on my conscience.

So here's how I see it:

We want the same thing.

I never want to kill anyone ever again.

And neither do you.

   (Beat.)

So how do we do that?

SHEILA. We say deal.

"Deal."

Now untie us and we can all go on our way.

AMI. Could you stop being so fucking patronizing?

I could have just left you here.

I still might.

But I am trying to figure out a way for us both to win.

SHEILA. Todd said you convinced him to start showing the property to investors again.

AMI. We had a huge fight about it, but I finally convinced him it was the right thing to do.

SHEILA. Why do you care?

AMI. Because I believe the glass is half-full.

> (**GLORIA** *opens her eyes. She urges* **SHEILA** *to be more aggressive.*)

SHEILA. How's the gluten-free diet going?

AMI. How do you know that?

SHEILA. Todd told me.

He told me all about you.

He told me about the games you play. To make up for lost time.

AMI. Like Pillow Fart?

SHEILA. He mentioned Pillow Fart, but he didn't tell me how to play.

AMI. It's when you fart into a pillow and then smother the other person's face with it.

It's gross.

SHEILA. It's probably been nice, right? To have a brother this past year.

AMI. It's been the best.

SHEILA. He told me about Embrace the Suck. We even played a game of it.

AMI. Who won?

SHEILA. He did.

> (**GLORIA** *opens her eyes again – urging* **SHEILA** *on.*)

You wanna play?

AMI. Sure.

How many people have you killed?

SHEILA. I thought we were going to play Embrace the Suck?

AMI. Oh, we already are.

How many people have you killed?

(Beat.)

Have you killed more than one person?

SHEILA. Yes.

AMI. I have killed only one person and it sucks.

Your turn.

SHEILA. Out of the corner of my eye, I keep seeing my sister's head blown apart – over and over.

It sucks.

AMI. Did Todd know it was coming?

Or did you just like – in the back of his head when he wasn't paying attention?

SHEILA. ...He knew it was coming.

AMI. Was he scared?

SHEILA. Yes.

...He wet his pants.

AMI. So have you.

(Beat.)

If you want to live, I need two things.

One: I need you to prove to me that you won't come after me.

Two –

SHEILA. What can I do to –

AMI. May I finish please?

Do you know how many times, every single day, people interrupt me?

Sometimes I keep track. You know what my record is?

Seventy-three times.

One day, I was interrupted – mid-sentence – seventy-three times. And that sucks.

SHEILA. I apologize for interrupting you. I suck.

AMI. One: I need you to prove to me that you won't come after me.

Two: You have to tell me who hired you.

Because I know they are gonna come after me.

As soon as I turn eighteen, I inherit half the company through the trust, and that information will then become public record.

SHEILA. You'll inherit it all now.

AMI. Oh.

> *(This is not a good thing to her.)*

Yeah.

...If I could sell the company and take all the money and go back in time to yesterday morning and give it all to you – for you to stop doing this – I would.

I would give anything for you to have filled up your tank, said hello to Tara Hutchinson, and never picked up a gun again.

SHEILA. How do you know about Tara?

AMI. 726-324-6644 is our fail-safe number.

When someone calls it, it splits the connection and keeps part of the line open – like leaving the phone off the hook.

I've heard everything you've said since you called it.

And I could track where you are.

SHEILA. You buried it in the concrete.

AMI. Yeah, but with the microphone just poking out – so I could hear you. But so you couldn't get to it.

And yes, I disabled Siri.

SHEILA. The battery would be dead by now.

AMI. It died a couple hours ago.

SHEILA. Where did you get a fail-safe number like that?

AMI. I made it.

SHEILA. How old are you?

AMI. Are we still playing Embrace the Suck?

SHEILA. We're still playing.

How old are you?

AMI. I'm seventeen. It sucks.

SHEILA. Who's the six-foot-two unemployed kindergarten teacher?

AMI. She's a six-foot-two unemployed kindergarten teacher. Just a decoy.

SHEILA. Are you really still in high school?

AMI. Yes.

It sucks.

SHEILA. Are you really on the scholastic bowl team?

AMI. Yes.

It's awesome. We won state last year.

Who was the first woman elected to the Senate?

SHEILA. I don't know.

AMI. Hattie Caraway in 1932.

What state?

Arkansas.

You know how many states have never elected a female senator?

SHEILA. I don't know – nine?

AMI. Twenty. Can you believe that? It is the twenty-first century and there are twenty states that have never elected a female senator. How hard does that suck?

Hashtag fuck the patriarchy. Am I right?

SHEILA. How the hell did we get outsmarted by a high schooler?

AMI. I'm gifted.

SHEILA. I can see that.

AMI. I've got so many AP credits, I'll be able to finish college in two-and-a-half years.

SHEILA. What do you want to be when you grow up?

AMI. A senator.

SHEILA. Good luck with that.

AMI. Thanks.

SHEILA. Better hope no one finds out you're a murderer.

AMI. I'm not a murderer.

SHEILA. Um –

AMI. What I did was just.

SHEILA. Every kill I have ever made has been just.

AMI. Todd didn't deserve to be killed.

SHEILA. Todd was a scumbag who wrecked hundreds of people's lives.

AMI. He was trying to change.

SHEILA. So am I.

AMI. You really suck at playing Embrace the Suck, you know that?

SHEILA. Well, maybe that's because who I'm playing with sucks.

AMI. I don't suck. You suck.

SHEILA. No, you suck.

AMI. You suck.

SHEILA. You suck.

AMI. You suck.

SHEILA. You suck.

AMI. You suck.

SHEILA. You suck.

AMI. It sucks that when I first walked in here, you looked right at me and only saw some dumb, harmless girl.

SHEILA. Yes, that sucks – but you used it to your advantage. Like I have used it to my advantage every day of my life.

> *(Beat.)*

What's your name? It's not Gabriella – what is it?

Your brother asked me to tell him my real name and I told him the truth.

What's your name?

AMI. Why did you tell him the truth?

SHEILA. Because I was going to kill him.

AMI. ...My name is Ami.

With an i. Not a y.

SHEILA. I'm Sheila.

AMI. You have to do like eleven more sucks before it's my turn again.

SHEILA. It sucks that I peed myself.

And it sucks that I have a UTI that's burning like crazy and itching and I'm tied to a chair.

It sucks that I'm so thirsty I can't think straight.

It sucks that you didn't bring me a latte.

It sucks that my sister and I will never get to watch *The Bachelor* together again.

It sucks that I work so much, I don't have any friends.

It sucks that you took my hacksaw because that's the hacksaw I used to cut through Gilbert Kolinski's ribs before I ripped out his heart.

*(**AMI** looks at the hacksaw in her hands.)*

AMI. You've like washed it since, right?

SHEILA. Yeah, I wash it every night before I go to sleep.

AMI. Really?

SHEILA. No.

AMI. Gross.

(She puts the hacksaw down on the ground. She takes out some Purell and puts it on her hands.)

Why did Gilbert Kolinski kill your dad?

SHEILA. Because he sucked.

AMI. Your dad or Gilbert Kolinski?

(Beat.)

Did your dad kill someone that Gilbert Kolinski loved?

SHEILA. My daddy was an insurance salesman.

AMI. ...So your mom killed someone that Gilbert Kolinski loved.

(Beat.)

And instead of killing your mom
he killed her husband.

So she'd feel what he felt.

So they'd be even.

So why wasn't it even?

SHEILA. Because Gilbert Kolinski killed my father.

> *(The plastic sheets on the windows breathe in and out.)*

Ever since I saw my father's face

in his casket

something knocked loose inside me.

And since that day,

I have killed over and over

and I have enjoyed doing it.

And that sucks.

That is the part of me I get from my mother.

But I also have a lot of my daddy in me.

And he was kind and gentle and strong.

He'd take moths that got inside our house, cup them in his hands, and let them loose outside.

I am

tired

of doing this.

Yesterday

something knocked loose inside you.

But what if it's not too late to put it back?

> *(AMI listens to the plastic breathing in and out.)*

AMI. ...When the air comes in and out

it sounds like the plastic is breathing.

Like the building is breathing in and out.

In

and out.

> *(They listen.)*

It almost sounds like a sleeping monster.

Somewhere below.

Don't wake it up.
Don't wake it back up.

> (**AMI** *and* **SHEILA** *breathe in with the building.*)
>
> (*They breathe out.*)

SHEILA. ...Is this who we want to be?
Or are we more than this?

> (*They breathe in together.*)
>
> (*They breathe out together.*)

Why don't we take one last look?
Why don't we look down our throats
past our hearts
and into our gut.

> (*The sound of the plastic breathing in and out.*)
>
> (*A few moments pass.* **AMI** *closes her eyes.*)

Do you see what's knocked loose?
Can you reach it?
Stretch as far as you can –
even if you think you can't reach it
just try to.
Can you reach it?

> (*They listen to the plastic move in and out.*)

AMI. Forgive us our trespasses,
as we forgive those who trespass against us.
Forgive us our trespasses,
as we forgive those who trespass against us.

> (*Beat.*)

Will you forgive me?

> (*Beat.* **AMI** *and* **SHEILA** *open their eyes and look at one another.*)

Because that's the only way you won't come after me,
right?

...If you actually, truly forgive me for what I did
and if I forgive you for what you did.
If you say it like you mean it
and tell me who hired you,
I will let you go.

> *(Beat.)*

Do you forgive me?

> *(Pause.)*

SHEILA. I...

> *(Pause.)*

AMI. Will you please forgive me?

> *(She waits for an answer.)*
>
> (**SHEILA** *tries to give her one, but can't.*)
>
> *(A long silence.)*
>
> *(Crestfallen,* **AMI** *starts to leave.)*

GLORIA. *(Loudly, startling both* **AMI** *and* **SHEILA**.*)* You know what sucks?

(In her normal voice.) To hear you two going on and on about forgiveness and what is just.

(Mockingly.) "Say it like you mean it. Say it like you mean it."

Give me a break.

Listen here, little girl –

AMI. My name is Ami.

GLORIA. "My name is Ami with an i not a y."

Well, Ami, let me break this down for you – and I know you're gifted so you'll be able to keep up.

All killing is wrong.

You can call it whatever you want, but it's all murder.

You murdered my daughter.

We murdered your brother.

And yeah, he was a scumbag – and maybe he was trying to be better – but who isn't trying to be better?

We're all *trying*.

But taking a life is never justified.

Never – in the history of the world – has there been a justifiable killing. Not-a-once.

And if you think you are righteous enough to decide who lives and who dies, then you're trying to play God.

And that's a game I don't care to play.

So I don't pretend to have any kind of morality – I just say:

Bang, bang, you're dead, ker-ching, ker-ching, on to the next.

I know where I'm going at the ding-dong of doom.

And sure – you can pretend, like Sheila here, to have a moral compass. But she's just fooling herself:

All three of us here – we're all going to hell in a handbasket.

SHEILA. Um –

GLORIA. So here's the deal, *Ami* – with an i,

either you are going to kill us – or you are not going to kill us. You have to decide that all on your own. There is nothing we can say that will change your mind.

So. What'll it be?

AMI. Do you promise not to kill me?

GLORIA. I thought you said you were gifted. Did you hear anything I just said?

AMI. Yes, I heard you, but I do not agree with you.

I vehemently disagree with both your outlook on the world

and your outlook on this particular situation.

It is not only up to me. We have to do this together. We have to be fucking Girl Scouts.

So I need to know:

Can you two be Girl Scouts? – can you *promise* to leave me alone if I let you go?

GLORIA. We promise.

(Beat.)

AMI. Who hired you?

GLORIA. Only Abi knows that.

AMI. She said you're the only one who knows.

GLORIA. She only said that so you didn't shoot me in the head.

AMI. I don't want to shoot you in the head.

GLORIA. Great – then stop yammering and untie us.

AMI. Who hired you?

GLORIA. I don't know! Dig up my daughter and ask her – she's the only one who knows, I swear to God.
I swear to God.
So either kill us or set us free. But this –
(Mocking her.) Waa waa waa promise me waa waa
is getting real tiresome.
Untie us.

(Beat.)

Untie us or pull the trigger.
If you don't untie us by the count of three, it means you're going to kill us.
Three.
Two.
One.
Bang, bang. That's it, Sheila. We're dead.
This girl is totally in over her head and she's freaking out and she's about to blow our brains out. I can see it in her eyes that she's a cold-blooded killer.

AMI. No, I'm not.

GLORIA. *(To AMI.)* Yes, you are and you know you are.
(To SHEILA.) This – right now – is bonus time.
It's nice that we can say goodbye.
But that's all this is.
Goodbye, Sheila. I love you.

SHEILA. This is not goodbye.

GLORIA. Say it!

Goodbye, my beautiful daughter. I love you.

SHEILA. I'm not gonna say shit.

GLORIA. *(To* **AMI**.*)* So stubborn. Even to the end.

Do you have a cigar?

Or a cigarillo?

AMI. What?

GLORIA. You said you smoked.

AMI. I have cigarettes.

GLORIA. I guess that'll have to do.

AMI. I'm not giving you a cigarette.

GLORIA. Pretty please with a cherry on top.

AMI. You killed my brother.

GLORIA. You killed my daughter – give me a cigarette!

> (**AMI** *takes out a pack of cigarettes and opens it. It's empty.*)

AMI. I'm out. Been chain-smoking for some reason.

GLORIA. Well, shit. I always wanted to have a smoke before I die.

Look to the sky. And then – curtains.

Quick. Painless. Don't know what hit me.

At least, Abi had that.

Say, there should be a bag of chips over there. By the windows. Well, by where there should be windows. Do you mind getting it?

It was Abi's last meal. And I want it to be mine as well. Before my ride to hell in a handbasket.

Please.

Please.

Please get the chips.

Please.

> (**AMI** *stands and looks for the bag of chips.*)

GLORIA. Thank you.

What were they, Sheila? Baked Lays. What kind?
Sour Cream and Onion.

SHEILA. Cheddar and Sour Cream.

GLORIA. Cheddar and Sour Cream Baked Lays – yum, yum.
You see them?

(**AMI** *picks up the bag. She looks inside.*)

AMI. They're smashed.

GLORIA. That's okay.

(**AMI** *pours some of the smashed chips onto her hand.*)

AMI. And there's like dirt on them.

GLORIA. That's okay. I want to share that with Abi. My last
meal.

AMI. I'm not untying you.

GLORIA. You don't need to. Just a taste.

(**AMI** *goes to* **GLORIA** *and holds the chips above her.*)

(**GLORIA** *opens her mouth.*)

(**AMI** *drops some pieces of chips. They miss* **GLORIA**'s *mouth.*)

Dammit, sorry.

(**AMI** *lowers her hand and drops more chips.* **GLORIA** *bites* **AMI**'s *right index finger as hard as she can.* **AMI** *screams in pain.*)

AMI. No, no, no, stop, stop, stop – my finger!

(**GLORIA** *bites* **AMI**'s *finger off.* **AMI** *screams. She clutches her bleeding hand.* **SHEILA** *struggles against her ropes.*)

(**GLORIA** *spits* **AMI**'s *finger onto the ground.*)

(**AMI** *puts* **GLORIA** *in a headlock. At the same time, she holds her bleeding hand as tightly as she can with her other hand.*)

Dammit! – that hurts.

GLORIA. You will –
> never –
> pull the –
> trigger –
> again!

>> *(The sound of a couple of crows – attracted by the chips.)*

>> *(**SHEILA** struggles so much against her ropes that her chair tips over.)*

>> *(She falls to the ground, facing away from **GLORIA** and **AMI**.)*

SHEILA. Dammit.

>> *(**AMI** readjusts her grip on her bleeding hand and her hand slips down by **GLORIA**'s mouth. **GLORIA** bites her other index finger.)*

AMI. No, no, no, let go, let it go.

>> *(**GLORIA** shakes her head no.)*

> Stop it, stop it. /

>> *(She slaps **GLORIA**.)*

>> *(**GLORIA** bites off her left index finger.)*

> Oh, God.

>> *(She stumbles away. She looks down at her bleeding hands.)*

> Oh, God.

SHEILA. / I can't see – what's happening?
> Mom? Are you okay?

>> *(**AMI** passes out.)*

> What's happening?

GLORIA. Th–

>> *(She spits **AMI**'s finger onto the ground.)*

> The power of positive thinking is what's happening.
> Ami? Ami? Hey, Cinderella?
> She's out.

SHEILA. Are you okay?

GLORIA. I prefer not to resort to biting off fingers – but I didn't see any other options.

SHEILA. Have you done it before?

GLORIA. Only once.

SHEILA. Are you kidding me?

GLORIA. No, no – twice before.

SHEILA. Cannibal.

GLORIA. It's not like I ate her fingers.

And I wasn't going for style-points – this was about survival.

SHEILA. Yeah, but –

GLORIA. Water is held by the shape of its container.

SHEILA. What?

GLORIA. Water is held by the shape of its container.

SHEILA. Are you saying we're the water or we're the container? Or is biting off the fingers the container?

GLORIA. Just think about it. You'll figure it out.

(*Beat.*)

SHEILA. Did you mean all that? – what you said?

GLORIA. Sure.

SHEILA. You think we're going to hell?

GLORIA. Oh, Sheila, you worry too much.

SHEILA. Mom –

GLORIA. It's what the girl needed to hear – in order to get her to give me a cigarette or some potato chips – so that I could bite off her finger.

What does it matter if I meant it or not?

SHEILA. But did you mean it?

GLORIA. A lady never tells the truth about her age or whether or not she thinks her daughter is going to hell.

(*Beat.*)

SHEILA. I love you, Mom.

GLORIA. I love you, kid.

SHEILA. I admire you so much.

GLORIA. Hold up! – don't start singing Kumbaya yet! We have to focus on getting out of here before Cinderella wakes up.

Did your ropes loosen up at all? – after you fell?

SHEILA. *(Struggling against her ropes.)* No.

GLORIA. You know what? I think if I just –

> *(She writhes up and down. Her chair begins to tip over.)*

Oh, crap, crap, crap –

> *(GLORIA and her chair fall sideways onto the floor.)*

Dammit.

SHEILA. What happened?

GLORIA. I'll give you one fucking guess.

> *(GLORIA and SHEILA are on the floor, still tied tightly to their chairs, facing away from each other.)*
>
> *(AMI is passed out, both hands covered in blood.)*

SHEILA. What about her cell phone? How far is she from you?

GLORIA. I can't see her anymore. She's off to my side. Only seven or eight feet, I think.

Okay, you scooch to where she dropped the hacksaw.

SHEILA. Where'd she drop it?

GLORIA. It's about five feet behind you.

I'll scooch to the girl. You scooch to the hacksaw.

We're in business again.

> *(They're still firmly tied to the chairs, but are now scooting on the floor.)*

(GLORIA seems to be moving a little better than SHEILA.)

SHEILA. It sounds like you're moving faster than me. What are you –

GLORIA. Focus on using your core. Lead with your core.

(They scoot.)

SHEILA. Oh.

That does make a difference.

I should've been doing that all along.

Wait – what are we going to do when we get there? How am I gonna pick up my hacksaw with my hands tied?

GLORIA. I don't know – you're just gonna rub up against the blade.

Besides, it's your lucky hacksaw, isn't it?

And me? – I'll dial the phone with my nose.

SHEILA. What about her passcode?

GLORIA. I'll start with 1, 2, 3, 4, 5, 6 and go from there.

SHEILA. But –

GLORIA. Water is held by the shape of its container – hee-yaw!

(They continue to scoot from their cores. They are moving just a little better.)

SHEILA. What did her finger taste like?

GLORIA. I did not eat her finger.

SHEILA. I only mean – what did it feel like – in your mouth?

GLORIA. I don't know what it felt like.

But it did remind me of how – on Thanksgiving when you try to pull a leg off the turkey – the only thing you really think is:

Gee, this is harder to get off than you think it'd be.

SHEILA. But –

GLORIA. No more talking – only scooting.

Cinderella is bound to wake up soon.

Let's do double-time. Double-time for Abi.

(They scoot in double-time. They still aren't getting far.)

SHEILA. I think you mean Sleeping Beauty.

GLORIA. What?

SHEILA. Cinderella was never like asleep.

GLORIA. Cinderella didn't sleep?

*(**AMI** comes to. Neither **GLORIA** or **SHEILA** can see her.)*

SHEILA. No, I just mean –

Never mind.

GLORIA. Abi's favorite Disney movie – go.

Aladdin.

SHEILA. No, it's *The Little Mermaid.*

(They scoot.)

Remember that Halloween she was Ariel?

She had me tie her feet together and wrap her legs in a green bedsheet?

(She tries to scoot like a mermaid.)

*(Still unseen, **AMI** picks up the gun.)*

(She awkwardly places her middle finger on the trigger.)

I was Flounder. I wore my yellow jumper.

*(She tries to scoot like a flounder. **GLORIA** continues to scoot.)*

You were Ursula. You let us paint you purple.

Daddy was King Triton.

You know what I'd give to go back to that day?

GLORIA. Don't look back, look forward.

*(**AMI** shoots **GLORIA** in the heart. **GLORIA** gasps in agony.)*

SHEILA. Mom?

Mom!

>   (**AMI** *goes to* **SHEILA** *and pushes her chair
>   around so that* **SHEILA** *can see* **GLORIA**. **GLORIA**
>   *soundlessly gasps.*)

No, no, no, no.

No! Mom!

AMI. *(To* **SHEILA**.*)* Why couldn't you let us be even?

SHEILA. Mom, I'm here. I love you.

AMI. *(To* **GLORIA**.*)* Why'd you bite off my fingers?

(To both **GLORIA** *and* **SHEILA**.*)* What is wrong with you
people?

SHEILA. *(To* **AMI**.*)* Be quiet!

(To **GLORIA**.*)* Mom, it's gonna be okay.

Everything is gonna be okay.

AMI. Why did you make me do this?

SHEILA. *(To* **AMI**.*)* Shut up!

>   (**AMI** *stops talking but starts pacing.*)

(To **GLORIA**.*)* I love you, Mom.

I couldn't have asked for a better mother.

>   (**GLORIA** *takes a belabored breath in.*)
>
>   *(Out.)*
>
>   *(Pause.)*
>
>   *(In.)*

(To **AMI**.*)* Stop pacing.

>   (**AMI** *stops pacing.*)
>
>   *(They listen.)*
>
>   (**GLORIA** *breathes out.*)

Goodbye, Mom.

I love you.

>   (**GLORIA** *takes a shallow breath in.*)
>
>   *(Then – nothing.)*

(SHEILA and AMI listen to the silence for several moments.)

AMI. What have I done?

I –

I don't feel right, I –

I can't look at her.

(She puts a tarp over GLORIA.)

(She coughs intentionally.)

(Quietly.) That's what the nurse at school told me. If you feel like you're going to pass out – cough.

(After finishing with the tarp, AMI stands before SHEILA.)

I didn't want this.

I didn't want any of this.

Todd was changing. He was trying to be better.

He actually, truly was.

He showed you the property because he was trying to fix this.

And you killed him!

You killed him for it!

(She raises the gun to SHEILA.)

Three.

SHEILA. *(Urgently.)* What do you get when you take a glass half-empty and add it to a glass half-full?

(Beat.)

(AMI keeps the gun aimed at SHEILA but doesn't fire it.)

Todd told me to tell you he's sorry that he loves you that you are not alone because you are brave and resourceful – he told me to ask you what do you get when you take a glass half-empty and add it to a glass half-full – he said you'd know what it means.

(Beat.)

SHEILA. What does it mean?

     (Beat.)

What do you get when you take a glass half-empty and add it to a glass half-full?

AMI. ...You get a full glass of water.

     (She lowers the gun.)

Todd, he...

He called me Half-Full.

And I called him Half-Empty.

And whenever we said goodbye, that's what we'd say to each other.

And then together, we'd go –

(Like after someone drinks a Coke.) Ahh.

     (Beat.)

SHEILA. What do you get when you take a glass half-empty and add it to a glass half-full?

AMI. A full glass of water.

SHEILA & AMI. Ahh.

     (Beat.)

SHEILA. Let me take you to the hospital.

Untie me and –

AMI. I can't untie you.

SHEILA. Then come over here.

I need to tell you something.

AMI. I don't care to lose any more fingers.

SHEILA. Come here and let me look at you.

Please, sister, come here – just for a moment.

     *(**AMI** gets down near **SHEILA**.)*

A little closer.

     *(**AMI** doesn't move closer. Her eyes start to close.)*

Hey, eyes open.

Cough.

*(**AMI** coughs and opens her eyes.)*

...Yesterday morning I was sent a message and I ignored it.

I saw two angels. And they warned me.

Two girls

braiding each other's hair

they looked me in the eyes

and they told me to stop.

(Quietly.) "Stop."

"Stop."

They said

from the backseat of Tara Hutchinson's Dodge Caravan.

"Stop."

And I should have stopped.

I should have walked away. And if I had, Abi and my mother would still be alive.

This is all my fault.

This is –

I am –

I –

> *(She writhes against her ropes, against the chair, against the floor. It is as though something is growing inside of her – as though she is cleansing the blood in her veins. Perhaps she gasps for air like a newborn.)*

I forgive you.

And I am sorry I killed your brother.

I am sorry I killed Gilbert Kolinski.

I am sorry.

Our Father, who art in heaven,

hallowed be thy name,

thy kingdom come.

Thy will be done on earth

as it is in heaven.

Give us this day our daily bread

and forgive us our trespasses,
as we forgive those who trespass against us.
Lead us not into temptation,
but deliver us from evil.
For thine is the kingdom, the power, and the glory,
Forever and ever.
Amen.

> *(Pause.)*

Leave here and never look back.

AMI. You'll die.

SHEILA. Go. Go right now.

> *(**AMI** gets her bag. She stops in front of **SHEILA**.)*

AMI. I forgive you.

> *(She leaves.)*

> *(**SHEILA** waits in silence.)*

> *(After several moments, **AMI** re-enters. She makes a beeline to **SHEILA** and starts to untie her.)*

SHEILA. *(Quietly.)* ..."Stop."

> *(**SHEILA** doesn't move. It's very difficult for **AMI** with her hands. It takes awhile, but eventually the ropes start to loosen.)*

"Stop."

> *(Beat.)*

"Stop."

> *(Beat.)*

These two angels said, "Stop."

> *(She unties the rest of the ropes herself. She stands up.)*

> *(**AMI** doesn't move. She doesn't raise her gun.)*

I'm gonna take you to the hospital, okay?
Maybe they'll be able to reattach your fingers.

AMI. Don't you have to put them in milk?

SHEILA. That's for teeth.

It's ice for severed fingers. We can pick some ice up at the Shell. It's right on the way.

AMI. I think it's prolly too late for the fingers.

...I mean, they've been on the floor and the floor in here is so dirty.

(*Gently,* **SHEILA** *takes the gun out of* **AMI**'s *hands.*)

SHEILA. Everything is going to be okay. Okay?

AMI. Okay.

(**SHEILA** *holds* **AMI**.)

(**AMI** *holds* **SHEILA**.)

SHEILA. Okay?

AMI. Okay.

SHEILA. (*Quietly singing.*)

She'll be comin' round the mountain
She'll be comin' round the mountain

(*She kisses the top of* **AMI**'s *head. She runs her hands through* **AMI**'s *hair as they continue to hold each other.*)

She'll be comin' round the mountain when she comes.
She'll be drivin' six white horses when she comes.
She'll be drivin' six white horses when she comes.

(*She shoots* **AMI** *in the head.*)

(**AMI** *slumps to the ground.*)

She'll be drivin' six white horses

(*She shoots* **AMI** *again and again – until the gun is empty.*)

She'll be drivin' six white horses
She'll be drivin' six white horses when she comes.

End of Play